ARTEMIS FOWL

THE SEVENTH DWARF

EOIN COLFER

PUFFIN

For Finn. Artemis's best friend

PUFFIN BOOKS

Published by the Penguin Group
Penguin Books Ltd, 80 Strand, London WC2R 0RL, England
Penguin Group (USA), Inc., 375 Hudson Street, New York, New York 10014, USA
Penguin Books Australia Ltd, 250 Camberwell Road, Camberwell, Victoria 3124, Australia
Penguin Books Canada Ltd, 10 Alcorn Avenue, Toronto, Ontario, Canada M4V 3B2
Penguin Books India (P) Ltd, 11 Community Centre, Panchsheel Park, New Delhi – 110 017, India
Penguin Books (NZ) Ltd, Cnr Rosedale and Airborne Roads, Albany, Auckland, New Zealand
Penguin Books (South Africa) (Pty) Ltd, 24 Sturdee Avenue, Rosebank 2196, South Africa

Penguin Books Ltd, Registered Offices: 80 Strand, London WC2R 0RL, England

www.penguin.com

First published 2004
1

The moral right of the author and illustrator has been asserted

Set in 12½/16 pt Monotype Perpetua
Typeset by Rowland Phototypesetting Ltd, Bury St Edmunds, Suffolk

Made and printed in England by
Mackays of Chatham plc, Chatham, Kent

British Library Cataloguing in Publication Data
A CIP catalogue record for this book is available from the British Library

ISBN 0–141–31800–7

www.eoincolfer.com

This section of the Lower Elements Police Artemis Fowl file is sealed and may not be accessed by anyone with less than alpha+ security clearance. The Fei Fei Affair occurred shortly after the fairy People's initial contact with Artemis Fowl. At this time, Artemis's mother had been returned to health by LEP Captain Holly Short, but his father was still missing, presumed dead, in Northern Russia.

CHAPTER ONE:
LADY FEI FEI'S TIARA

Below the Fleursheim Plaza. Manhattan. New York City.

Dwarfs dig tunnels. That's what they are born to do. Their bodies have adapted over millions of years to make them efficient tunnellers. A dwarf male's jaw can be unhinged, so that he can unhook it at will in order to excavate a tunnel with his mouth. The waste is jettisoned at the rear end to make way for the next mouthful.

The dwarf that concerns us, is the notorious fairy

felon Mulch Diggums. Mulch found burglary much more suited to his personality than mining. The hours were shorter, the risks were less severe, and the precious metals and stones that he took from the mud men were already processed, forged and polished.

Tonight's target was the tiara of Lady Fei Fei, a legendary Chinese diplomat. The tiara was a masterpiece of intricate jade and diamond arrangements in a white gold setting. It was priceless, though Mulch would sell it for much less.

The tiara was currently on tour as the centrepiece of an Oriental art exhibition. On the evening our story begins, it was overnighting in the Fleursheim Plaza on its way to the Classical Museum. For one night only, Fei Fei's tiara was vulnerable and Mulch did not intend to miss his chance.

Incredibly, the original geological planning survey for the Fleursheim Plaza was freely available on the Internet, allowing Mulch to plot his route from the comfort of the East Village where he was holed up. The dwarf discovered, to his delight, that a narrow vein of compacted clay and loose shale ran right up to the basement wall. The basement where the Fei Fei Tiara was being stored.

At that moment, Mulch was closing his jaws around five kilos of earth per second as he burrowed ever closer to the Fleursheim basement. His hair and beard resembled an electrified halo as each sensitive fibre tested the surface for vibrations.

It wasn't bad clay, Mulch mused as he swallowed, taking shallow breaths through his nostrils. Breathing and swallowing simultaneously is a skill lost by most creatures once they leave infancy, but for dwarfs it is essential for survival.

Mulch's beard hair detected vibration close by. A steady thrumming that usually indicated air conditioning units or a generator. That didn't necessarily mean he was nearing his target. But Mulch Diggums had the best internal compass in the business, plus he'd programmed the precise coordinates into the stolen Lower Elements Police helmet in his knapsack. Mulch paused long enough to check the 3D grid in the helmet's visor. The Fleursheim basement was forty eight degrees north east. Ten metres above his present position. A matter of seconds for a tunnel dwarf of his calibre.

Mulch resumed his munching, scything through the clay like a fairy torpedo. He was careful only to expel clay at the lower end, and not air. The air may be needed if he encountered any obstacles. Seconds later he encountered the very barrier he had been saving up for. His skull collided with six inches of basement cement. Dwarf skulls may be tough, but they cannot crack half a foot of cement.

'D'Arvit!' swore Mulch, blinking cement flakes from his eyes with long dwarf lashes. He reached up, rapping a knuckle against the flat surface.

'Five or six inches, I reckon,' he said to no one, or so he thought. 'Should be no problem.'

Mulch backed up, compacting the earth behind him. He was about to employ a manoeuvre known in dwarf culture as the *cyclone*. This move was generally used for emergency escapes or for impressing dwarf females. He jammed the unbreakable LEP helmet over his wild hair, drawing his knees to his chin.

'I wish you could see this, ladies,' he muttered, allowing the gas in his insides to build. He had swallowed a lot of air in the past few minutes, and now individual bubbles were merging to form an increasingly difficult to contain, tube of pressure.

'A few more seconds,' grunted Mulch, the pressure bringing a glow to his cheeks.

Mulch crossed his arms over his chest, drew in his beard hair, and released the pent-up wind.

The result was spectacular and would have earned Mulch the girlfriend of his choice, if anyone had been around to see it. If you imagine the tunnel to be the neck of a champagne bottle, then Mulch was the cork. He shot up that passageway at over a hundred miles per hour, spinning like a top. Ordinarily when bone meets cement, the cement wins, but Mulch's head was protected by a stolen fairy Lower Elements Police helmet. These helmets are made from a virtually indestructible polymer.

Mulch punched through the basement floor in a flurry of cement dust and spinning limbs. The dust was whipped into a dozen mini-whirlwinds by his jet stream. His momentum took him a full six feet into the air before he flopped to the floor, and lay there panting. The *cyclone* took a lot out of a person. Who said crime was easy?

After a quick breather, Mulch sat up and re-hinged his jaw. He would have liked a longer rest but there could be cameras pointed at him right now. There was probably a scrambler on the helmet, but technology had never been his strong point. He needed to nab the tiara, and escape underground.

He stood, shaking a few lumps of clay from his bum flap, and took a quick look around. There were no telltale red lights winking on cctv cameras. There were no safety-deposit boxes for valuable artefacts. There wasn't even a particularly secure door. It seemed an odd place for a priceless tiara to be stored even for one night. Humans were inclined to protect their treasures, especially from other humans.

Something winked at him from the darkness. Something that gathered in and reflected the minuscule amount of light available in the basement. There was a plinth among the statues, storage crates and mini-skyscrapers of stacked chairs. And atop the plinth was a tiara, and the spectacular blue stone at its centre glittered even in almost total darkness.

Mulch burped in surprise. The mud men had left Fei Fei's tiara out in the open? Not likely. This must be a set-up.

He approached the plinth cautiously, wary of any traps on the ground. But there was nothing, no motion sensors, no laser eyes. Nothing. Mulch's instinct screamed at him to flee, but his curiosity pulled him towards the tiara like a swordfish on a line.

'Moron,' he said to himself, or so he thought. 'Get out while you can. Nothing good can come of this.' But the tiara was magnificent. Mesmerizing.

Mulch ignored his misgivings about the situation, admiring the jewelled headdress in front of him.

'Not half bad,' he said, or maybe it was. The dwarf leaned closer.

The stones had an unnatural sheen to them. Oily. Not clean like real gems. And the gold was too shiny. Nothing a human eye would notice. But gold is life to a dwarf. It is in their blood and dreams.

Mulch lifted the tiara. It was too light. A tiara of this size should weigh at least two pounds.

There were two possible conclusions to be drawn from all this. Either this was a decoy and the real tiara was safely hidden elsewhere, or this was a test, and he had been lured here to take that test. But lured here by whom? And for what purpose?

These questions were answered almost immediately. A giant Egyptian sarcophagus popped open in the deepest of the shadows, revealing two figures who were most definitely not mummies.

'Congratulations, Mulch Diggums,' said the first, a pale boy with dark hair. Mulch noticed that he wore night vision goggles. The other was a giant bodyguard who Mulch had humiliated recently enough for it to still smart. The man's name was Butler, and he did not look in the best of moods.

'You have passed my test,' continued the boy, in confident tones. He straightened his suit jacket and stepped from the sarcophagus extending a hand.

'A pleasure to meet you. Mister Diggums, I am your new business partner. Allow me to introduce myself. My name is . . .'

Mulch shook the hand. He knew who this boy was. They had battled before, just not face to face. He was the only human to ever have stolen fairy gold, and managed to keep it. Whatever he had to say, Mulch was certain that it would be interesting.

'I know who you are, Mud Boy,' said the dwarf. 'Your name is Artemis Fowl.'

CHAPTER TWO:
HIGH PRIORITY.

Police Plaza. Haven City. The Lower Elements.

When Mulch Diggums said the name *Artemis Fowl*, the Mud Boy's file was automatically shunted to the hot pile in Police Plaza. Every fairy Lower Elements Police helmet was fitted with a satellite tracker and could be located anywhere in the world. They also had voice activated microphones, so whatever Mulch said was heard by a surveillance intern. The case was immediately removed from the intern's desktop when Artemis's name was mentioned. Artemis Fowl was fairy enemy number one, and anything related to the Irish boy was sent immediately to the LEP's technical adviser, the centaur, Foaly.

Foaly logged on to the live transmission from Mulch's helmet, and cantered into LEP Commander Root's office.

'We have something here, Julius. It could be important.'

Commander Julius Root looked up from the fungus cigar he was clipping. The elf did not look happy, but then he rarely did. His complexion was not as rosy as usual, but the centaur had a feeling that was about to change.

'A few words of advice, pony boy,' snapped Root, tearing the tip from the cigar. 'One, don't call me Julius. And two, there is a protocol in place for speaking to me. I'm the commander here, not one of your polo buddies.'

He leaned back in his chair, lighting the cigar. Foaly was unimpressed by all the posturing.

'Whatever. This is important. Artemis Fowl's name has come in on a sound file.'

Root sat up abruptly, protocol forgotten. Less than a year previously Artemis Fowl had kidnapped one of his captains, and extorted half a ton of gold from the LEP ransom fund. But more important than the gold itself was the knowledge inside the Irish boy's head. He knew of the People's existence, and might decide to exploit them again.

'Talk quickly, Foaly. No jargon, just Gnommish.'

Foaly sighed. Half the fun of delivering vital news was explaining how his technology had made gathering the news possible.

'OK. A certain amount of LEP hardware goes missing every year.'

'Which is why we can remote destruct them.

'In most cases, yes.'

The commander's cheeks flushed angrily. 'Most cases, Foaly? You never said anything about *most cases* during the budget meeting.'

Foaly raised his palms. 'Hey, you try to remote destruct it if you like. See what happens.'

The commander glared at him suspiciously. 'And why shouldn't I just press the button right now?'

'Because the self-destruct has been switched off, meaning someone clever has got hold of it. Previously the helmet was active, which means someone was wearing it. We couldn't risk blowing off a fairy's head, even if he or she is a criminal.'

Root chewed the butt of his cigar. 'I'm tempted, believe me. Where did this helmet come from? And who is wearing it?'

Foaly consulted a computer file on the com-card in his palm. 'It's an old model. Best guess, a surface fence sold it to a rogue dwarf.'

Root crushed the cigar into an ash tray. 'Dwarfs. If they're not mining protected areas, they're stealing from the humans. Do we have a name?'

'No. The distance is too great to run a voice pattern analysis. Anyway, even if we could, as you know, due to the unique positioning of their larynx, all dwarf males have basically the same voice.'

'This is all I need,' groaned the commander. 'Another dwarf on the surface. I thought we'd seen the last of that when . . .' He paused, saddened by a sudden memory. The dwarf Mulch Diggums had been killed months earlier, tunnelling out of Artemis Fowl's manor. Mulch had been a huge pain in the rear end, but he hadn't been without charisma.

'So, what do we know?'

Foaly read from a list on his screen. 'Our unidentified subject burrows into a Manhattan basement, where he meets Artemis Fowl Junior. Then they leave together, so something is definitely up.'

'What is up, exactly?'

'We don't know. Fowl knew enough about our technology to turn off the mike, and the self-destruct, probably because Butler took a load of equipment from LEP retrieval during the Fowl Manor siege.'

'What about global positioning? Did Artemis know enough to turn that off?'

Foaly grinned smugly. 'That can't be turned off. Those old helmets had a tracker layer sprayed on.'

'How fortunate for us. Where are they now?'

'In Fowl's jet, heading for Ireland. It's a Lear, top of the range.' Foaly noticed the commander's laser stare. 'But you probably don't care about the jet, so let's move on shall we?'

'Yes, let's,' said Root caustically. 'Do we have anyone topside?'

Foaly activated a large plasma screen on the wall, quickly negotiating his way through files to a world map. There were fairy icons pulsing in various countries.

'We have three Retrieval teams but nobody in the old country.'

'Naturally,' groaned Root. 'That would be far too handy.' He paused. 'Where's Captain Short?'

'On vacation above ground. I would remind you that she's off field duty, pending a tribunal.'

Root waggled his fingers at imaginary regulations. 'Minor detail. Holly knows Fowl better than any fairy alive. Where is she?'

Foaly consulted his computer, as if he didn't already know. As if he didn't make a dozen calls from his workstation every day, to see if Holly had picked up that hoof-moisturiser he'd asked for.

'She's in the Cominetto Spa. I don't know about this, Commander. Holly is tough, but Artemis Fowl kidnapped her. Her judgement could be clouded.'

'No,' said Root. 'Holly is one of my best officers, even if she doesn't believe it. Get me a line to that spa. She's going back to Fowl Manor.'

CHAPTER THREE:
THE 7TH DWARF

The Island of Cominetto. Off the coast of Malta.
The Mediterranean.

The Cominetto Spa was the most exclusive holiday destination for the People. It took several years of repeated application to get visa approval for a visit, but Foaly had done a little computer hocus pocus to get Holly on the shuttle to the Spa. She needed the break after what she'd been through. And was still going through. For now, instead of giving her a medal for saving half of the ransom fund, LEP Internal Affairs were actually investigating her.

In the past week, Holly had been exfoliated, laser peeled, purged (don't ask) and tweezered within an inch of her life, all in the name of relaxation. Her coffee-coloured skin was smooth and blemish free, and her cropped auburn hair glowed with internal lustre. But she was bored out of her skull.

The sky was blue, the sea was green and the living was easy. And Holly knew that she would go completely berserk if she had to spend one more minute being pampered. But Foaly had been so pleased when he had set this trip up, that she didn't have the heart to tell him how fed up she was.

Today she was lying in a bubble pool of algae sludge have her pores rejuvenated and playing *guess the crime*. This was a game where you assumed that everyone that passed by was a criminal, and you had to guess what they were guilty of.

The white-suited algae therapist wandered over with a phone on a transparent platter.

'A call from Police Plaza, Sister Short,' he said. His tone left Holly in no doubt what he thought of phone calls in this oasis of calm.

'Thank you, Brother Hummus,' she said, snatching the handset. Foaly was on the other end.

'Bad news, Holly,' said the centaur. 'You've been recalled to active duty. A special assignment.'

'Really?' said Holly, simultaneously punching the air and trying to sound disappointed. 'What's the assignment?'

'Take a couple of deep breaths,' advised Foaly. 'And maybe a few pills.'

'What is it, Foaly?' insisted Holly, though her gut already knew.

'It's . . .'

'Artemis Fowl,' said Holly. 'I'm right, aren't I?'

'Yes,' admitted Foaly. 'The Irish boy is back. And he's teamed up with a dwarf. We don't know what they're planning, so you need to find out.'

Holly clambered from the sludge tub, leaving a trail of green algae on the white carpet.

'I can't imagine what they are planning,' she said, bursting into the locker room. 'But I can tell you two things. We won't like it, and it won't be legal.'

The Fowl Lear Jet. Over the Atlantic Ocean

Mulch Diggums was soaking in the Lear jet's high spec Jacuzzi bath. He absorbed gallons of water through his thirsty pores, flushing the toxins from his system. When he felt sufficiently refreshed, he emerged from the bathroom wrapped in an oversized bathrobe. He looked like nothing more than the world's ugliest bride, trailing a train behind him.

Artemis Fowl was toying with an iced tea while he waited for the dwarf. Butler was flying the plane

Mulch sat at the coffee table, pouring an entire saucer of nuts down his gullet, shells and all.

'So, Mud Boy,' he said. 'What's going on in that devious brain of yours?'

Artemis steepled his fingers, peering around them

through wide-set blue eyes. There was quite a lot going on in his devious mind, but Mulch Diggums would only be hearing a small portion of it. Artemis did not believe in sharing all the details of his schemes with anyone. Sometimes the success of these plans depended on nobody knowing exactly what they were doing. Nobody but Artemis himself.

Artemis put on his friendliest face, leaning forward in his chair.

'The way I see it, Mulch,' he said. 'You already owe me a favour.'

'Really, Mud Boy? And how do you figure that?'

Artemis patted the LEP helmet on the table beside him. 'No doubt you bought this on the black market. It is an older model, but it still has the standard LEP voice activated mike, and self-destruct.'

Mulch tried to swallow the nuts, but his throat was suddenly dry.

'Self-destruct?'

'Yes. There's enough explosive packed in here to turn your head to jelly. There would be nothing left but teeth. Of course there would be no need to activate the self-destruct, if the voice activated mike leads the LEP right to your door. I have switched these functions off.'

Mulch frowned. He would be having words with the fence who sold him the helmet.

'OK. Thanks. But you don't expect me to believe that you saved me out of the goodness of your heart.'

Artemis chuckled. He could hardly expect anyone who knew him to believe that.

'No. We have a common goal. The Fei Fei Tiara.'

Mulch folded his arms across his chest. 'I work alone. I don't need you to help me steal the tiara.'

Artemis plucked a newspaper from the table, spinning it across to the dwarf. 'Too late, Mulch. Someone already beat us to it.'

The headline was in bold capitals: CHINESE TIARA STOLEN FROM CLASSICAL.

Mulch frowned. 'I'm getting a bit confused here, Mud Boy. The tiara was at the Classical? It was supposed to be at the Fleursheim.'

Artemis smiled. 'No, Mulch. The tiara was never at the Fleursheim. That was just what I needed you to believe.'

'How did you know about me?'

'Simple,' replied Artemis. 'Butler told me of your unique tunnelling talents, so I began to research recent robberies. A pattern began to emerge. A series of jewellery robberies in New York state. All subterranean entries. It was a simple matter to lure you to the Fleursheim by planting some misinformation at Arty Facts, the website you get your data from. Obviously, with the special talents you displayed at Fowl Manor, you would be invaluable to me.'

'But now someone else has stolen the tiara.'

'Exactly. And I need you to recover it.'

Mulch sensed that he had the upper hand. 'And why would I want to recover it? And even if I did, why would I need you, human?'

'I need precisely that tiara, Mulch. The blue diamond on its crown is unique, in hue and quality. It will form the basis for a new laser I am developing. The rest of the tiara will be yours to keep. We would be a formidable team. I plan, you execute. You will live out your exile in total luxury. This first job will be a test.'

'And if I say no?'

Artemis sighed. 'Then I will post my information concerning your being alive and your whereabouts on the Internet. I'm sure LEP Commander Root, will stumble on it eventually. Then I fear, your exile will be short lived, and completely devoid of luxury.'

Mulch jumped to his feet. 'So it's blackmail is it?'

'Only if it has to be. I prefer cooperation.'

Mulch felt his stomach acid bubble. Root thought he had died during the Fowl Manor siege. If the LEP found out that he was alive, then the commander would make it his personal mission to put him behind bars. He didn't have much choice.

'OK, human. I'll do this job. But no partnership.

One job only, then I disappear. I feel like going straight for a couple of decades.'

'Very well. It's a bargain. Remember, if you ever change your mind, there are many so-called impregnable vaults in the world.'

'One job,' insisted Mulch. 'I'm a dwarf. We work alone.'

Artemis took a plan sheet from a tube, spreading it on the table.

'That's not strictly true, you know,' he said, pointing to the first column on the sheet. 'The tiara was stolen by dwarfs, and they have been working together for several years. Very successfully too.'

Mulch crossed the room, reading the name above Artemis's finger.

'Sergei the Significant,' he said. 'I think someone has an inferiority complex.'

'He's the leader. There are six dwarfs in Sergei's little band, collectively known as the Significants,' continued Artemis. 'You are to be the seventh.'

Mulch giggled hysterically. 'Of course, why not? The seven dwarfs. This day started off badly, and my beard hair tells me that it's about to get a whole lot worse.'

Butler spoke for the first time. 'If I were you, Mulch,' he said in his deep gravelly tones. 'I'd trust the hair.'

*

Holly was out of the spa as soon as she had hosed the algae from her skin. She could have taken a shuttle back to Haven, then caught a connecting flight, but Holly preferred to fly.

Foaly contacted her on her helmet intercom as she skipped across the Mediterranean wave tops, trailing her fingers in the spume.

'Hey, Holly, did you get that hoof cream?'

Holly smiled. No matter what the crisis, Foaly never lost sight of his priority: Himself. She dipped the flaps on her wings, rising to a hundred feet.

'Yes, I got it. It's being couriered down. There was a *buy one get one free* deal on. So expect two tubs.'

'Excellent. You have no idea how hard it is do get good moisturiser below ground. Remember, Holly, this is between us. The rest of the guys are still a bit old fashioned when it comes to cosmetics.'

'Our little secret,' said Holly reassuringly. 'Now, do we have any idea yet what Artemis is up to?'

Holly's cheeks reddened at the mere mention of the Mud Boy's name. He had kidnapped her, drugged her and ransomed her for gold. And just because he'd had a change of heart at the last minute, deciding to let her go, didn't mean all was forgiven.

'We don't know exactly what's going on,' admitted Foaly. 'All we know is that they must be up to no good.'

'Any video?'

'Nope. Audio only. And we don't even have that any more. Fowl must have disconnected the mike. All we have left is the tracker.'

'What are my orders?'

'The Commander says to stick close, plant a bug if you can, but under no circumstances make contact. That is Retrieval's job.'

'OK. Understood. Surveillance only, no contact with the Mud Boy or the dwarf.'

Foaly opened a video window in Holly's visor, so she could see the scepticism on his face. 'You say that as if the very idea of disobeying an order is unheard of for you. If I remember correctly, and I think I do, you've been on report a dozen times for ignoring your superiors.'

'I wasn't ignoring them,' retorted Holly. 'I was taking their opinions under advisement. Sometimes only the officer on the spot can take the proper decision. That's what being a field agent is all about.'

Foaly shrugged. 'Whatever you say, Captain. But if I were you, I'd think twice before going against Julius on this one. He had that look on his face. You know the one.'

Holly terminated the link with Police Plaza. Foaly didn't need to explain further. She knew the one.

CHAPTER FOUR:
SHOWTIME

The Circus Maximus. Wexford Racecourse.
Southern Ireland.

Artemis, Butler and Mulch had ringside seats for the Circus Maximus. This was one of a new breed of circus where the acts lived up to the advertising, and there were no animals involved. The clowns were genuinely funny, the acrobats were little short of miraculous and the dwarfs were little and short.

Sergei the Significant and four of his five teammates were lined up at the centre of the ring, doing a spot of pre-show posturing to the capacity crowd. Each dwarf was below a metre in height and wore a tight-fitting crimson leotard with lightning flash logo. Their faces were concealed by matching masks.

Mulch was wrapped in an oversized raincoat. He wore a peaked hat pulled over his brow, and his face was slathered with a pungent homemade sun block. Dwarfs are extremely photosensitive with a burn-time of mere minutes, even in overcast conditions.

Mulch poured an entire jumbo carton of popcorn down his gullet.

'Yep,' he mumbled, spitting out kernels. 'These boys are actual dwarfs, no doubt about it.'

Artemis smiled tightly, glad to have his suspicions confirmed. 'I discovered them quite by accident. They use the same website you do.'

'My computer search revealed two patterns, and it was easy to match the circus's movements to a series of crimes. I am surprised that Interpol and the FBI aren't already on to Sergei and his gang. When the Fei Fei Tiara's tour schedule was announced, and it coincided with the circus tour, I knew it was no chance coincidence. I was, of course, correct. The dwarfs stole the tiara, then smuggled it back to Ireland using the circus as cover. Actually it will be far easier to steal the tiara from these dwarfs, that it would have been from the Classical.'

'And why is that?' asked Mulch.

'Because they are not expecting it,' explained Artemis.

Sergei the Significant and his troupe prepared for their first trick. It was as simple as it was impressive. A small unadorned wooden box was lowered by crane into the centre of the ring. Sergei, with much bowing and flexing of tiny muscles, made his way towards the box. He lifted the lid and climbed in. The cynical audience waited for some curtain or screen shenanigans that would allow the little man to escape, but nothing happened. The box sat there. Immobile. With every eye in the tent drilling into its surface. Nobody went within twenty feet of it.

A full minute passed before a second dwarf entered the ring. He set an old fashioned T-bar detonator on the ground, and following a five-second drum roll, pushed the plunger. The box exploded in a dramatic cloud of soot and balsa wood. Either Sergei was dead, or he was gone.

'Hmmph,' grunted Mulch, amidst the thunderous applause. 'Not much of a trick.'

'Not when you know how it's done,' agreed Artemis.

'He gets in the box, he tunnels out to the dressing room, and presumably he shows up again later.'

'Correct. They set down another box at the end of the performance, and lo-and-behold, Sergei reappears. It's a miracle.'

'Some miracle. All the talents we have, and that's the best those bums could come up with.'

Artemis rose, Butler instantly stood behind him,

to block any possible attack from the rear. 'Come, Mister Diggums, we need to plan for tonight.'

Mulch swallowed the last of the popcorn. 'Tonight? What's tonight?'

'Why the late evening performance,' replied Artemis with a grin. 'And you, my friend, are the star performer.'

Fowl Manor. North County Dublin. Ireland.

It was a two-hour drive back to Fowl Manor from Wexford. Artemis's mother was waiting for them at the front doors.

'And how was the circus, Arty?' she said, smiling for her boy, in spite of the pain in her eyes. That pain was never far away, not even since the fairy, Holly Short, cured her of her depression following the disappearance of her husband, Artemis's father.

'It was fine, mother. Wonderful in fact. I asked Mister Diggums here for dinner, he is one of the performers and a fascinating fellow. I hope you don't mind.'

'Of course not. Mister Diggums, make the house your own.'

'It wouldn't be the first time,' muttered Butler under his breath. He escorted Mulch through to the kitchen while Artemis lingered to talk with his mother.

'How are you, Arty, really?'

Artemis did not know how to respond. What was he to say? I have determined to follow in my father's criminal footsteps, because that is what I do best. Because that is the only way to raise enough money to pay the numerous private detective agencies and Internet search companies that I have employed to find him. But the crimes don't make me happy. Victory is never as sweet as I think it will be.

'I am fine, Mother, really,' he said eventually, without conviction.

Angeline hugged him close. Artemis could smell her perfume and feel her warmth.

'You're a good boy,' she sighed. 'A good son.'

The elegant lady straightened. 'Now, why don't you go and talk to your new friend. You must have a lot to discuss.'

'Yes, Mother,' said Artemis, his resolve overcoming the sadness in his heart. 'We have a lot to discuss before tonight's show.'

The Circus Maximus. Wexford Racecourse.
Southern Ireland.

Mulch Diggums had cleared himself a hole just below the dwarfs' tent and was waiting to spring into action. They had returned to Wexford for the late-night performance. Early enough for him to dig his way under the tent from an adjacent field. Artemis was inside the main tent right now keeping a close eye on Sergei the Significant and his team. Butler was hanging back by the rendezvous point, waiting for Mulch's return.

Artemis's scheme had seemed plausible back in Fowl Manor. It had even seemed likely that they could get away with it. But now, with the circus vibrations beating down on his head, Mulch could see a slight problem. The problem being that he was putting his neck on the line, while Mud Boy was sitting in a comfy ringside seat eating candy floss.

Artemis had explained his scheme in Fowl Manor's drawing room.

'I have been keeping close tabs on Sergei and his troupe ever since I discovered their little outfit. They are a canny group. Perhaps it would be easier to steal the gem from whoever they sell the stone on to, but soon the school holidays will be over, and I will be forced to suspend my operations, so I need the blue diamond now.'

'For your laser thing?'

Artemis coughed into his hand. 'Laser. Yes, that's correct.'

'And it has to be this diamond?'

'Absolutely. The Fei Fei blue diamond is unique. Its precise hue is one of a kind.'

'And that's important is it?'

'Vital, for light diffraction. It's technical. You wouldn't understand it.'

'Hmm,' droned Mulch, suspecting that something was being held back. 'So how do you propose we get this vital blue diamond?'

Artemis pulled down a projector screen. There was a diagram of the Circus Maximus taped to the surface.

'Here is the circus ring,' he said, pointing with a telescopic pointer.

'What? That round thing, with the word ring in the middle? You don't say.'

Artemis closed his eyes, breathing deeply. He was unaccustomed to interruptions. Butler tapped Mulch on the shoulder.

'Listen, little man,' he advised in his most serious voice. 'Or I might remember that I owe you a ignominious beating, like the one you gave me.'

Mulch swallowed. 'Listen, yes, good idea. Do continue, Mud Boy . . . em, Artemis.'

'Thank you,' said Artemis. 'Now. We have been observing the dwarf troupe for months and in all that time, they have never left their own tent unguarded, so we presume that this is where they keep their loot. Generally the entire group are there, except during a performance when five of the six are needed for the acrobatic routine. Our only window of opportunity is during this period when all but one of the dwarfs are in the ring.'

'All but one?' enquired Mulch. 'I can't be seen by anybody. If they so much as catch a glimpse of me, they'll hunt me down forever. Dwarfs really hold a grudge.'

'Let me finish,' said Artemis. 'I have put some thought into this, you know. We managed to obtain some video one evening in Brussels from a pencil camera that Butler poked through the canvas.'

Butler turned on a flat-screen television and pressed play on a video remote. The picture that appeared was grey and grainy, but perfectly recognizable. It showed a single dwarf in a round tent, lounging in a leather armchair. He was dressed in the Significants' leotard and mask and was blowing bubbles through a small hoop.

The earthen floor began to vibrate slightly in the centre of the tent where the ground looked disturbed, as though a small earthquake was disrupting that spot only. Moments later a metre diameter circle of earth collapsed entirely, and a masked Sergei emerged from the hole. He vented some gas, and gave his comrade the thumbs up. The bubble-blowing dwarf immediately ran out of the tent.

'Sergei has just tunnelled out of his box, and our bubble-blowing friend is needed in the ring,' explained Artemis. 'Sergei takes over guard duty until the end of the act, when all the other dwarfs return and Sergei reappears in the new box. We have approximately seven minutes to find the tiara.'

Mulch decided to pick a few holes in the plan. 'How do we know the tiara is even there?'

Artemis was ready for that question. 'Because my sources tell me that there are five European jewellery fences coming to tonight's show. They are hardly here to see the clowns.'

Mulch nodded slowly. He knew *where* the tiara would be. Sergei and his significant friends would hide everything a few metres below their tent, safely buried beyond the reach of humans. That still left hundreds of square metres to search.

'I'll never find it,' he pronounced eventually. 'Not in seven minutes.'

Artemis opened his Powerbook laptop. 'This is a computer simulation. You are the blue figure. Sergei is the red figure.'

On screen the two computer creatures burrowed through simulated earth.

Mulch watched the blue figure for over a minute.

'I have to admit it, Mud Boy' said the dwarf. 'It's clever. But I need a tank of compressed air.'

Artemis was puzzled. 'Air? I thought you could breathe underground?'

'I can.' The dwarf grinned hugely at Artemis. 'It's not for me.'

So now, Mulch sat in his underground hole with a diver's tank of air strapped to his back. He squatted absolutely silently. Once Sergei entered the earth, his beard hair would be sensitive to the slightest vibration, including radio transmissions, so Artemis had insisted on radio silence until they were in phase two of the plan.

To the west, one high frequency vibration punched through the ambient noise. Sergei was making his move. Mulch could feel his brother dwarf scything through the earth, possibly towards his secret cache of stolen jewellery.

Mulch concentrated on Sergei's progress. He was tunnelling east, but on a downward tangent, obviously heading directly for something. The sonar in Mulch's beard hair fed him constant speed and direction updates. The second dwarf proceeded at a steady pace and incline for almost a hundred metres, then stopped dead. He was checking something. Hopefully the tiara.

Following half a minute of minimal movement, Sergei made for the surface, almost directly for Mulch. Mulch felt a sheen of sweat coat his back. This was the dangerous part. He reached slowly into his leotard, pulling out a ball the size and colour of a satsuma. The ball was an organic sedative used by Chilean natives. Artemis had assured Mulch that it had no side effects, and would actually clear up any sinus problems Sergei may have.

With infinite care, Mulch positioned himself as close to Sergei's trajectory as he dared, then wiggled the fist containing the sedative ball into the earth. Seconds later, Sergei's scything jaws consumed the ball along with a few kilo's of earth. Before he had taken half a dozen bites, his forward motion slowed to a dead halt, and his chewing grew sluggish. Now was the dangerous time for Sergei. If he was left unconscious with a gut full of clay, he could choke. Mulch ate through the thin layer of earth separating them, he flipped the sleeping dwarf on to his back, feeding an air tube deep into the black depths of his cavernous mouth. Once the tube was in place, he twisted the tank's nozzle, sending a sustained jet of air through Sergei's system. The air stream ballooned the little fairy's internal organs, flushing all traces of clay through his system. His body shook as though connected to a live wire, but he did not awaken. Instead he snored on.

Mulch left Sergei curled in the earth, and aimed his chomping jaws towards the surface. The clay was typical Irish, soft and moist with low level pollution and teeming with insect life. Seconds later, he felt his questing fingers break the surface, cool air brushing across their tips. Mulch made sure that the circus mask covered the upper half of his face, then pushed his head above ground.

There was another dwarf sitting in the armchair. Today he was playing with four yo-yos. One spinning from each hand and each foot. Mulch said nothing, though he felt a sudden longing to chat with his fellow dwarf. He simply gave a thumbs-up signal.

The second dwarf coiled in his yo-yos wordlessly. Then pulling on a pair of pointy toed boots, bolted for the tent flap. Mulch could hear the sudden roar of the crowd as Sergei's box exploded. Two minutes gone. Five minutes left.

He upended his rear and plotted a course for the exact spot where Sergei had stopped. This was

33

not as difficult as it would seem. Dwarfs' internal compasses are fantastic instruments, and can lead the fairy creatures with the same accuracy as any GPS system. Mulch dived.

There was a small chamber hollowed out below the tent. A typical dwarf hidey hole, with spit slickened walls providing low level luminescence in the darkness. Dwarf spit is multi-functional secretion. Apart from the normal uses, it also hardens on prolonged contact with air to form a lacquer, that is not also tough but also slightly luminous.

Sitting in the centre of the small chamber was a wooden chest. It was not locked. Why would it be? There would be no one down here but dwarfs. Mulch felt a stab of shame. It was one thing robbing from the mud men, but he was ripping off brother dwarfs who were just trying to make an honest living stealing from humans. It was an all time low. Mulch made up his mind to somehow reimburse Sergei the Significant and his band once this was over.

The tiara was inside the chest, the blue stone on its crown winked in the light of the spittle. Now there was a real jewel. Nothing fake about that. Mulch stuffed it inside his leotard. There were plenty of other jewels in the box, but he ignored them. It was bad enough taking the tiara. Now all he had to do was haul Sergei to the surface where he could recover safely, and leave the same way he had come. He would be gone before the other dwarfs realized anything was wrong.

Mulch headed back towards Sergei, collected his limp form and ate his way back to the surface, dragging his sleeping brother dwarf behind him. He re-hinged his jaw, climbing from the hole.

The tent was still deserted. The Significants should be well over half way through their act by now. Mulch dragged Sergei to the lip of the hole, and took a dwarf flint dagger from his boot. He would cut some strips from the chair and secure Sergei's hands, feet and jaws. Artemis had assured him that Sergei would not wake up, but what did the Mud Boy know about dwarf insides.

'Sorry about this, brother,' he whispered almost fondly. 'I hate to do it, but the Mud Boy has me over a barrel.'

Something shimmered in the corner of Mulch's vision. It shimmered and then spoke.

'First I want you to tell me about the Mud Boy, dwarf,' it said. 'And then I want you to tell me about the barrel.'

CHAPTER FIVE:
RINGMASTER

Holly Short flew north until she came to mainland Italy, then turned forty degrees right over the lights of Brandish.

'You are supposed to avoid major flight routes and city areas,' Foaly reminded her over the helmet speakers. 'That is the first rule of recon.'

'The first rule of recon is to find the rogue fairy,' Holly retorted. 'Do you want me to locate this dwarf or not? If I stick to the coastline, it will take me all night to reach Ireland. My way, I'll get there by eleven p.m. local time. Anyway, I'm shielded.'

Fairies have the power to increase their heart rate and pump their arteries to bursting, which causes their bodies to vibrate so quickly that they are never in one place long enough to be seen. The only human ever to see through this magical trick, pardon the pun, was, of course, Artemis Fowl, who had filmed fairies on a high speed camera then viewed the frames still by still.

'Shielding isn't as foolproof as it used to be,' noted Foaly. 'I have sent the helmet's tracker pattern to your helmet. All you have to do is follow the beep. When you find our dwarf, the commander wants you to . . .'

The centaur's voice faded out in a liquid hiss of static. The magma flares beneath the earth's crust were up tonight, whiting out LEP communications. This was the third time since she started the journey. All she could do was proceed according to plan, and hope the channels cleared up.

It was a fine night, so Holly navigated using the stars. Of course her helmet had a built-in GPS triangulated by three satellites, but stellar navigation was one of the first courses taught in the LEP academy. It was possible that a recon officer could be trapped above ground without science, and under those circumstances the stars could be that officer's only hope of finding a fairy shuttle port.

The landscape sped by below her, dotted by an ever growing number of human enclaves. Each time she ventured topside, there were more. Soon there would be no countryside left, and no trees to make the oxygen. Then everyone would be breathing artificial air above ground and below it.

Holly tried to ignore the pollution alert logo flashing in her visor. The helmet would filter out most of it, and anyway she had no choice. It was either fly over the cities, or possibly lose the rogue dwarf. And Captain Holly Short did not like to lose.

She enlarged the search grid in her helmet visor, and zeroed in on a large, circular, striped tent. A circus. The dwarf was hiding in a circus. Hardly original, but an effective place to pose as a human dwarf.

Holly dipped the flaps on her mechanical wings, descending to twenty feet. The tracker beep pulled her off to the left, away from the main tent itself, towards a smaller adjacent one. Holly swooped lower still, making sure to keep her shield fully buzzed up as the area was teeming with humans.

She hovered above the tip of the tent pole. The stolen helmet was inside, no doubt about it. To investigate further, she would have to enter the structure. The fairy bible, or Book, prevented fairies from entering human dwellings uninvited, but recently the high court had ruled that tents were temporary structures and as such were not included in the Book's edict. Holly burnt the stitches on the tent's seam with a laser burst from her Neutrino 2000, and slipped inside.

On the earthen surface below were two dwarfs. One had the stolen helmet strapped across his back, the second was jammed down a hole in the ground. Both wore upper face masks and matching red leotards. Very fetching.

This was a surprising development. Dwarfs generally stuck together, yet these two seemed to be playing for different teams. The first appeared to have incapacitated the second, and perhaps was about to go even further. There was a glittering flint dagger in his hand. And dwarfs did not generally draw their weapons unless they intended to use them.

Holly toggled the mike switch on her glove. 'Foaly? Come in Foaly? I have a possible emergency here.'

Nothing. White noise. Not even ghost voices. Typical. The most advanced communications system in this galaxy, and possibly a few others, all rendered useless by a few magma flares.

'I need to make contact, Foaly. If you can record this, I have a crime in process, possibly murder. Two fairies are involved, there is no time to wait for Retrieval. I'm going in. Send Retrieval immediately.'

Holly's good sense groaned. She was already technically off active duty, making contact would bury her Recon career for certain. But ultimately that didn't matter. She had joined the LEP to protect the People, and that was exactly what she intended to do.

She set her wings to descend, floating down from the tent shadows.

The dwarf was talking, in that curious gravelly voice common to all male dwarfs.

'Sorry about this, brother,' he said, perhaps making excuses for the impending violence. 'I hate to do it, but the Mud Boy has me over a barrel.'

Enough, thought Holly. There will be no murder here today. She unshielded, speckling into view in a fairy shaped starburst. 'First I want you to tell me about the Mud Boy,' she said. 'And then I want you to tell me about the barrel.'

Mulch Diggums recognized Holly immediately. They had met only months previously in Fowl Manor. Funny how some people were fated to meet over and over. To be part of one another's lives.

He dropped both the dagger and Sergei, raising empty palms. Sergei slid back down the hole.

'I know what this looks like, Ho . . . officer. I was just going to tie him up, for his own good. He had a tunnel convulsion, that's all. He could hurt himself.'

Mulch congratulated himself silently. It was a good lie and he had bitten his tongue before it could utter Holly's name. The LEP thought he had died in a cave in, and she would not recognize him with the mask. All Holly could see was silk and beard.

'A tunnel convulsion? Dwarf kids get those, not experienced diggers.'

Mulch shrugged. 'I'm always telling him. Chew your food. But will he listen? He's a grown dwarf, what can I do? I shouldn't leave him down there, by the way.' The dwarf put one foot into the tunnel.

Holly touched down. 'One more step, dwarf,' she warned. 'For now, tell me about the Mud Boy.'

Mulch attempted an innocent smile. There was more chance of a great white shark pulling it off. 'What Mud Boy, officer?'

'Artemis Fowl,' snapped Holly. 'Start talking. You're going to jail, dwarf. For how long depends on you.'

Mulch chewed it over for a moment. He could feel the Fei Fei Tiara pricking his skin beneath the leotard. It had slipped around the side, below the armpit, most uncomfortable. He had a choice to make. Try to complete the job, or look after number one. Fowl or a reduced sentence. It took less than a second to decide.

'Artemis wants me to steal the Fei Fei Tiara for him. My . . . ah . . . circus mates had already taken it, and he bribed me to pass it on to him.'

'Where is this tiara?'

Mulch reached inside his leotard.

'Slowly, dwarf.'

'OK. Two fingers.'

Mulch drew the tiara from under his armpit.

'You don't take bribes I suppose?'

'Correct. This tiara goes back near enough to wherever it came from. Police will get an anonymous tip and find it in a skip.'

Mulch sighed. 'The old skip routine. Don't the LEP ever get tired of that?'

Holly did not want to be drawn into conversation.

'Toss it on the ground,' she instructed. Then get down there yourself. Lie on your back.'

One did not order a dwarf to lie on the ground on his belly. One click of the jaws, and the perpetrator would be gone in a cloud of dust.

'On my back? That's really uncomfortable with this helmet.'

'On your back!'

Mulch obeyed, dropping the tiara and shifting the helmet to the front. The dwarf was thinking furiously. How much time had gone by? Surely the Significants would be back any second. They would come running to relieve Sergei.

'Officer, you really should get out of here.'

Holly searched him for weapons. She unstrapped the LEP helmet, rolling it across the floor.

'And why is that?'

'My teammates will be here any second. We're on a tight schedule.'

Holly smiled grimly. 'Don't worry about it. I can handle dwarfs. My gun has a nuclear battery.'

Mulch swallowed, glancing through Holly's legs towards the tent flaps. The Significants had arrived right on time, and three were sneaking through the tent flap making less noise than ants in slippers. Each dwarf held a flint dagger in his stubby fingers. Mulch heard a rustling overhead, and looked up to see another Significant peering through a fresh rip in the tent seam. Still one unaccounted for.

'The battery isn't important,' said Mulch. 'It's not how many bullets you have, it's how fast you can shoot.'

Artemis was not enjoying the circus. Butler should have contacted him over a minute ago to confirm that Mulch had arrived at the rendezvous point. Something must be wrong. His instinct told him to take a look, but he ignored it. Stick to the plan. Give Mulch every possible second.

The last few seconds ran out moments later when the five dwarfs in the ring took their bows. They exited the ring with a series of elaborate tumbles, and headed for their own tent.

Artemis raised his right fist to his mouth. Strapped

across his palm was a tiny microphone, of the type used by US secret service. A skin-tone earpiece was lodged in his right ear.

'Butler,' he said softly, the mike was whisper sensitive. 'The Significants have left the building. We must execute plan B.'

'Roger,' said Butler's voice in his ear.

Of course there was a plan B. Plan A may have been perfect, but the dwarf executing it certainly wasn't. Plan B involved chaos and escape, hopefully with the Fei Fei Tiara. Artemis hurried along his row while the second box was lowered into the centre of the ring. All around him, children and their parents cooed at the melodrama unfolding before them, unaware of the very real drama that was being played out not twenty metres away.

Artemis approached the dwarfs' tent, sticking to the shadows.

The Significants trotted ahead of him in a group. In seconds they would enter the tent and find that things were not as they should be. There would be delays and confusion, in which time the jewel merchants in the big top would probably come running, along with their armed security. This mission would either have to be completed or aborted in the next few seconds.

Artemis heard voices from inside the tent.

The Significants heard them too and froze. There shouldn't be voices. Sergei was alone, and if he was not, something was wrong. One dwarf crawled on his belly to the flap, peeking inside. Whatever he saw obviously upset him, because he crawled rapidly back to the group, and began issuing frantic instructions. Three dwarfs went in the front flap, one scaled the tent wall, and the other popped his bum flap and went subterranean.

Artemis waited a couple of heartbeats, then crept to the tent flap. If Mulch was still in there, something would have to be done to get him out, even if it meant sacrificing the diamond. He flattened his body against the tightly drawn canvas and peered inside. He was surprised by what he saw. Surprised but not amazed, he should have expected it really. Holly Short was standing over a fallen dwarf who may or may not have been Mulch Diggums. The Significants were closing in on her, daggers drawn.

Artemis raised the radio to his mouth.

'Butler, how far away are you, exactly?'

Butler answered immediately. 'I'm on the circus perimeter. Forty seconds, no more.'

In forty seconds, Holly and Mulch would be dead. He could not allow that.

'I have to go in,' he said tersely. 'When you get here, moderate plan B as necessary.'

Butler did not waste time arguing. 'Roger. Keep them talking Artemis. Promise them the world, and everything under it. Greed will keep you alive.'

'Understood,' said Artemis, stepping into the tent.

'Well well well,' said Derph, Sergei's second in command. 'Looks like the law finally tracked us down.'

Holly planted a foot on Mulch's chest, pinning him to the earth. She trained her weapon on Derph.

'That's right, I'm with Recon, Retrieval are seconds away. So just accept it and lie on your backs.'

Derph casually tossed his dagger from hand to hand. 'I don't think so, elf. We've been living this life for five hundred years, and we don't plan to stop now. You just let Sergei go, and we'll be on our way. No need for anyone to get hurt.'

Mulch realized that the other dwarfs believed he was Sergei. Maybe there was still a way out.

'Just stay where you are,' Holly ordered with more bravado than she felt. 'It's guns against knives here, you can't possibly win.'

Derph smiled through his beard. 'We've already won,' he said.

With the kind of synchronization born of centuries of teamwork, the dwarfs attacked together. One dropped from the shadows in the tent's upper regions, while another breached the earthen flooring, jaws wide, tunnel wind driving him a full three feet into the air. The vibration of Holly's voice had drawn him to her, as a struggling swimmer's kicks will draw a shark.

'Look out!' screeched Mulch, unwilling to let the Significants deal with Holly, even at the price of his own freedom. He may be a thief, but he realized that that was as low as he was willing to go.

Holly looked up, squeezing off a shot that stunned the descending dwarf, but she did not have time to look down. The second attacker clamped his fingers around her gun, almost taking the hand with it, then wrapped his powerful arms around Holly's shoulder's, squeezing the air from her body. The others closed in.

Mulch hopped to his feet.

'Wait, brothers. We need to interrogate the elf, find out what the LEP know.'

Derph didn't agree. 'No, Sergei. We do as we always do. Bury the witness and move on. Nobody can catch us underground. We take the jewels and go.'

Mulch punched the bear-hugging dwarf under the arm, a nerve cluster for dwarfs. He released Holly, and she fell gasping to the earth.

'No,' he barked. 'I am the pack leader here! This is an LEP officer. We kill her and a thousand more will be on our trail. We bind her and leave.'

Derph tensed suddenly, levelling the tip of his dagger at Mulch. 'You are different, Sergei. All this talk of sparing elves. Let me see you without the mask.'

Mulch backed up a step. 'What are you saying? You can see my face later.'

'The mask! Now! Or I'll see your innards as well as your face.'

And suddenly Artemis was in the tent, striding across the floor as if he owned the space.

'What is going on here?' he demanded, his accent decidedly German.

All faces turned to him. He was magnetic.

'Who are you?' asked Derph.

Artemis snorted. 'Who am I the little man asks. Did you not invite my master here from Berlin? My name is not important. All you need to know is that I represent Mister Ehrich Stern.'

'M–M–Mister Stern, of course,' stammered Derph. Ehrich Stern was a legend in the field of precious stones and how to dispose of them illegally. He also disposed of people who disappointed him. He had been invited to the tiara's auction and was sitting in row three, as Artemis well knew.

'We come here to do business, and instead of professionalism we find some kind of dwarf feud.'

'There is no feud,' said Mulch, still playing the part of Sergei. 'Just a little misunderstanding. We are deciding how to dispose of an unwelcome guest.'

Again, Artemis snorted. 'There is only one way to dispose of unwanted guests. As a special favour, we will perform that service for you, for a discount on the tiara of course.' He paused in disbelief, his eyes widening. 'Tell me this is not she,' he said, picking the tiara off the ground where Holly had dropped it. 'She lies in the dirt like some cluster of common stones. This truly is a circus.'

'Hey, take it easy,' said Mulch.

'And what is this?' demanded Artemis, pointing to Mulch's helmet in the dirt.

'I dunno,' said Derph. 'It's an LEP . . . I mean, the intruder's helmet. It's her helmet.'

Artemis waggled a finger. 'I think not, unless your tiny intruder has two heads. She is already wearing a helmet.'

Derph did the maths. 'Hey, that's right. So where did that helmet come from?'

Artemis shrugged. 'I just got here, but I would guess that you have a traitor in your midst.'

The dwarfs turned, as one, towards Mulch.

'The mask!' growled Derph. 'Take it off! Now!'

Mulch shot Artemis a look through the mask's eyeholes. 'Thanks a bunch.'

49

The dwarfs advanced in a semi-circle, knives raised.

Artemis stepped in front of the group. 'Halt, little men,' he said imperiously. 'There is only one way to save this operation, and that is certainly not by staining the earth with blood. Leave these two to my bodyguard, and then we shall commence negotiations.'

Derph smelled a rat. 'Wait a minute. How do we know you're with Stern? You waltz in here just in time to save these two. It's all a bit convenient if you ask me.'

'That's why nobody asks you,' retorted Artemis. 'Because you're a dullard.'

Derph's dagger glittered dangerously. 'I've had it with you, kid. I say we get rid of *all* witnesses and move on.'

'Fine,' said Artemis. 'This charade is beginning to bore me.' He raised his palm to his mouth. 'Time for plan B.'

Outside the tent, Butler wrapped the tent's mainstay around his wrist and pulled. He was a man of prodigious strength, and soon the metal pegs began to slide from the mud that held them. The canvas cracked, rippling and ripping. The dwarfs gaped at the billowing canvas.

'The sky is falling,' screamed a particularly dense one.

Holly took advantage of the sudden confusion, grabbing a stun grenade on her belt. She had seconds left before the dwarfs cut their losses and went subterranean. Once that happened it was all over. Nothing could catch a dwarf below ground. By the time Retrieval got here, the dwarfs would be miles away.

The grenade was strobe operated, sending out flashing light at such high frequency that too many messages were sent simultaneously to the watcher's brain, shutting it down temporarily. Dwarfs were particularly susceptible to this kind of weapon, as they had a low light tolerance in the first place.

Artemis noticed the silver orb in Holly's hand.

'Butler,' he said into his mike. 'We need to get out of here! Now. Northeast corner.'

He grabbed Mulch's collar, leading him backwards. Overhead the canvas was falling, its descent cushioned by trapped air.

'We go,' screamed Derph. 'We go now. Leave everything and dig.'

'You're not going anywhere,' gasped Holly, her breath rasping along a bruised windpipe. She twisted the timer, rolling the grenade into the midst of the Significants. It was the perfect weapon against dwarfs. Shiny. No dwarf can resist anything shiny. Even Mulch was watching the glittering sphere, and would have kept watching until the flash, had Butler not slit a five-foot gash in the canvas and yanked the pair through the gap.

'Plan B,' he grunted. 'Next time we pay more attention to the back-up strategy.'

'Recriminations later,' said Artemis briskly. 'If Holly is here, then back up won't be far away. There must have been some kind of tracker on the helmet, something he hadn't detected. Perhaps in one of the coatings.

'Here's the new plan. With the arrival of the LEP, we must split up now. I will write you a cheque for your share of the tiara. One point eight million euros, a fair black market price.'

'A cheque? Are you joking?' objected Mulch. 'How do I know I can trust you, Mud Boy?'

'Believe me,' said Artemis. 'I am not to be trusted, generally. But we made a deal, and I don't cheat my partners. Your could, of course, wait here for the LEP to arrive and discover your miraculous recovery from the usually fatal affliction of death.'

Mulch snatched the offered cheque. 'If this doesn't clear. Then I'm coming to Fowl Manor, and remember I know how to get in.' he noticed Butler's angry glare. 'Though obviously, I hope it doesn't come to that.'

'It won't. Trust me.'

Mulch unbuttoned his bum flap. 'It better not.' he winked at Butler. And he was gone, below the earth in a flurry of dust, before the bodyguard could respond. It was just as well really.

Artemis closed his fist around the blue diamond on the tiara's crown. It was already loose in its setting. All he had to do now was leave. Simple. Let the LEP clean up their own mess. But even before he heard Holly's voice, Artemis knew that it couldn't be that easy. Nothing ever was.

'Don't move, Artemis,' said the fairy captain. 'I won't hesitate to shoot you. In fact, I'm quite looking forward to it.'

Holly activated the Polaroid filter on her visor just before the stun grenade detonated. It was difficult to concentrate enough to perform even that simple operation. The canvas was flapping, the dwarfs were popping their bum flaps, and from the corner of her eye she noticed Fowl disappearing through a slit in the tent.

He would not escape again. This time she would get a mind-wipe warrant and erase the fairy People from the Irish boy's memory permanently.

She closed her eyes, in case any strobe light squeezed past her visor, and waited for the pop. The flash, when it came, lit up the tent like a lampshade.

Several seams of weak stitching were burnt out, and bands of white light shot skywards like wartime searchlights. When she opened her eyes, the dwarfs were unconscious on the tent floor. One was the unfortunate Sergei who had managed to climb from his tunnel just in time to get knocked out. Holly searched her belt for a Sleeper/Seeker hypodermic. The hypodermic contained small tracker beads loaded with a charged sedative. When the beads were injected into a fairy's bloodstream, that fairy could be tracked anywhere in the world, and knocked out at will. It made retrieving rogue fairies a lot easier. Holly quickly fought her way through the folds of canvas, tagged all six dwarfs, then crawled to the flaps. Now Sergei and his band could be apprehended at any time. This left her free to pursue Artemis Fowl.

The tent was around her ears now, held up by pockets of trapped air. She had to get out, or it would completely collapse on her. Holly activated the mechanical wings on her back, creating her own little wind tunnel, and hovered through the flap, boots scraping the earth.

Fowl was leaving along with Butler.

'Don't move, Artemis,' she yelled. 'I won't hesitate to shoot you. In fact, I'm quite looking forward to it.'

This was fighting talk, brimming with bravado and confidence. Two things that were in short supply, but at least she sounded ready for a fight.

Artemis turned slowly. 'Captain Short. You don't look so well. Maybe you should get some medical attention.'

Holly knew she looked terrible. She could feel her fairy magic healing the bruises on her ribs, and her vision was still jumpy from stun grenade overspill.

'I'm fine, Fowl. And even if I'm not, the computer in my helmet can fire this gun all on its own.'

Butler took a step to one side splitting the target. He knew Holly would have to shoot him first.

'Don't bother, Butler,' said Holly. 'I can drop you and hunt the Mud Boy down in my own time.'

Artemis tutted. 'Time is something you don't have. The circus hands are already coming. In seconds they will be here, followed closely by the circus audience. Five hundred people all wondering what is going on here.'

'So what? I'll be shielded.'

'So there is no way for you to take me in. And even if you could, I doubt that I have broken any fairy law. All I did was to steal a human tiara. Surely the LEP don't get involved in human crime. I can't be held responsible for fairy criminals.'

Holly struggled to keep her gun hand steady.

Artemis was right, he hadn't done anything to threaten the People. And the shouts from the circus folk were growing louder.

'So you see Holly, you have no choice but to let me go.'

'And what about the other dwarf?'

'What dwarf?' said Artemis innocently.

'The seventh dwarf. There were seven.'

Artemis counted on his fingers. 'Six I believe. Only six. Perhaps in all the excitement . . .'

Holly scowled behind her mask. There must be something she could salvage from this.

'Give me that tiara. And the helmet.'

Artemis rolled the helmet across the ground. 'The helmet, certainly. But the tiara is mine.'

'Give it to me,' shouted Holly, authority in every syllable. 'Give it to me, or I will stun you both and you can take your chances with Ehrich Stern.'

Artemis almost smiled. 'Congratulations, Holly. A masterstroke.' He took the tiara from his pocket, tossing it to the LEP officer.

'Now you can report that you broke up a gang of dwarf jewel thieves, and recovered the stolen tiara. A clutch of feathers in your cap, I would think.'

People were coming. Their thumping feet jarred the earth.

Holly set her wings to hover.

'We'll meet again, Artemis Fowl,' she said, rising into the air.

'I know,' replied Artemis. 'I look forward to it.'

It was true. He did.

Artemis watched his nemesis lift slowly into night sky. And just as the crowd appeared around the corner, she vibrated out of the visible spectrum. Only a fairy shaped patch of stars remained.

Holly really makes things interesting, he thought, closing his fist around the stone in his pocket. *I wonder if she will notice the switch. Will she look closely at the blue diamond and see that it seems a little bit oily.*

Butler tapped him on the shoulder.

'Time to be gone,' said the giant manservant.

Artemis nodded. Butler was right, as usual. He almost felt sorry for Sergei and the Significants. They would believe themselves safe right up until the Retrieval squad arrived to take them away.

Butler took his charge by the shoulder, and directed him to the shadows. In two steps they were invisible. Finding the darkness was a talent of Butler's.

Artemis looked skywards one last time. *Where is Captain Short now,* he wondered. In his mind she would always be there, looking over his shoulder, waiting for him to slip up.

EPILOGUE: FOWL MANOR.

Angeline Fowl sat slumped at her dressing table, tears gathering at the corners of her eyes. Today was her husband's birthday. Little Arty's father. Missing for over a year, and every day made his return more unlikely. Each day was difficult, but this day was almost impossible. She ran a slender finger over a photograph on the dresser. Artemis senior, with his strong teeth and blue eyes. Such a startling blue, she had never seen quite that colour before or since, except in the eyes of her son. It had been the first thing she had noticed about him.

Artemis entered the room hesitantly. One foot outside the threshold.

'Arty, dear,' said Angeline, drying her eyes. 'Come here. Give me a hug, I need one.'

Artemis crossed the deep pile carpet, remembering the many times he had seen his father framed by the bay window.

'I will find him,' he whispered once in his mother's arms.

'I know you will, Arty,' replied Angeline, fearful of the lengths her extraordinary son would go to. Afraid to lose another Artemis.

Artemis drew back. 'I have a gift for you, Mother. Something to remind you, and give you strength.'

He drew a golden chain from his breast pocket. Swinging in its V was the most incredible blue diamond. Angeline's breath caught in her throat. 'Arty, it's uncanny. Amazing. That stone is exactly the same colour . . .'

'As father's eyes,' completed Artemis, coupling the clasp around his mother's neck. 'I thought you might like it.'

Angeline gripped the stone tightly in her hand, the tears flowing freely now. 'I shall never take it off.'

Artemis smiled sadly. 'Trust me, Mother, I will find him.'

Angeline looked at her son in wonder. 'I know you will, Arty,' she said again. But this time, she believed it.

A remote network connection has uncovered an e-mail
containing new information about Eoin Colfer

| New | Save | Print | Open | Close | Send | Reply | Address Book | De |

From   Eoin Colfer   Status   Confiden

What rocks my world:

1. Wife and family. Of course, what else did you think
   would be number one?
2. Coming home from a long trip.
3. Heavy metal music. AC/DC are the kings. Although
   new band, The Darkness, are after their crown.
4. The sea. Waves, foam, blowholes. The business.
5. A night at the cinema. Give me a good blockbuster for tw
   hours of escapism. 'Cause you don't get much of that
   writing about leprechauns.
6. Apple computers. So cool and shiny. Aaah.
7. Stand-up comedy. Har de har har. Oh stop it,
   I can't take any more.
8. Ireland. The people, the colours, lovely.
9. Writing.
10. Meeting my readers. Yes, it's really me. What do
    you mean, you thought I'd be taller?

What makes me feel fowl:

1. Onions, also garlic. We'll count that as one.
   A stinky-vegetables category.
2. Queues. Bank, supermarket, airports. You name it, I hate it.
3. Leaks. Roof, boat, pants.
4. Arguing. No you don't. Yes I do. Shut up! Don't
   you tell me to shut up ... etc.
5. Doing the ironing, especially shirts. Baby clothes
   are quite tricky too.
6. Feeding the baby at 5 a.m. Though he does manipulate me
   into liking him with his cute gurgling.
7. Loneliness. Being alone stinks. In fairness I don't get
   much of it, but after ten minutes I start blubbering.
8. Good looking, athletic people who are also smart and nice
   Highly unfair. Nature is supposed to share out the gifts
9. Accounting – numbers and figures, it's all blah blah blah
   to me.
10. Gremlins. They come into your house at 5 a.m and eat all
    your Jaffa Cakes ... No, hold on, that was me during the
    5 a.m baby feed. I apologize unreservedly to gremlins
    everywhere.

To find out more about Eoin Colfer click to:
eoincolfer.com, puffin.co.uk or artemisfowl.co.uk